Kate Salvino
Madison Salvino

For Olivia

The photographer would like to thank
the following children for making this book possible:
Adam, Alex, Chris, Emma, Felix, Jacob, Jo, Laura,
Mikael, Olivia, Sally, Sophie, Taffa, and Tessa.
Thanks are also due to Bristol Zoo, Snakes n' Stuff
and Park House Farm

Text and photographs copyright © 1996 by David Ellwand

CIP Data is available.

First published in the United States 1997
by Dutton Children's Books,
a division of Penguin Books USA Inc.
375 Hudson Street, New York, New York 10014

Originally published in 1996 by
Ragged Bears Limited, Hampshire, England
Typography by Ellen M. Lucaire
Printed in Hong Kong
First American Edition
ISBN 0-525-45792-5
2 4 6 8 10 9 7 5 3 1

EMMA'S

ELEPHANT

& Other Favorite Animal Friends

DAVID ELLWAND

Dutton Children's Books · New York

Rachel's rascally rat,

Simon's slithery snake,

Carla's cute calf,

David's
dotted
dog.

Gail's gorgeous guinea pig,

Bella's beautiful butterfly,

Ricky's relaxed rabbit,

and Priscilla's pretty pig.

Sam's slimy snails,

Caroline's
contented
cockatoo,

Pete's perfect pony,

and Terry's terrific turkey.

Catherine's cuddly cat

and
Gordon's
glittering
goldfish.

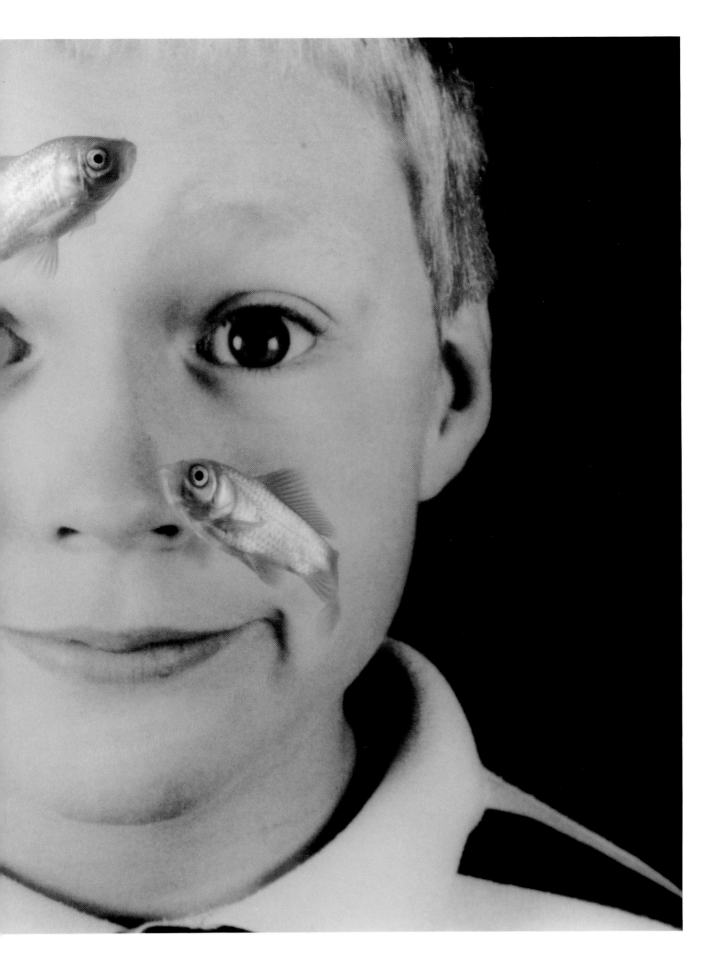

But nothing is as *big* as...

Emma's ENORMOUS

elephant!

Madison Salvidea